Chan and his Van

Written by Jenny Roberts

Illustrated by Nicola Anderson

Collins

Chan has a van.

3

This fan belongs to Jan.

The hats belong to Max.

Ding, dong!

This backpack belongs to Jack.

This quill belongs to Will.

Ding, dong!

11

This fish belongs to Tish.

/j/

14

/v/

15

After reading

Letters and Sounds: Phase 3

Word count: 40

Focus phonemes: /j/ /v/ /w/ /x/ /qu/ /ch/ /sh/ /th/ /ng/ /nk/

Common exception words: and, the, to

Curriculum links: Personal, Social and Emotional Development

Early learning goals: Reading: read and understand simple sentences; use phonic knowledge to decode regular words and read them aloud accurately; read some common irregular words

Developing fluency

- Your child may enjoy hearing you read the book.
- Ask your child to read the sentences with expression, using a bell-like voice for **ding** and **dong**, and emphasising the words that rhyme, such as **fan** and **Jan** on page 4.

Phonic practice

- Focus on **Thanks** on page 13. Ask your child to find the pairs of letters that each make one sound. (/th/ and /nk/)
- Ask your child to find the two letters that make one sound in each of these words:

  Chan ding dong belongs backpack Jack
- Challenge your child to identify pairs of letters that make one sound in **quill** on page 10. (qu/i/ll)
- Look at the "I spy sounds" on pages 14–15 together. Point to the children jumping on the trampoline and say "jump", emphasising the /j/ sound. Point to the van and say "van", emphasising the /v/ sound. Challenge your child to find more words containing these sounds. Explain that the sound can be in the middle or end of the words, too. (e.g. *jet, joggers*; *vehicle*)

Extending vocabulary

- Focus on the repeated /ng/ sound in **ding** and **dong**. Challenge your child to think of another /ng/ word with the same meaning and ending. (e.g. *bing, tring*)
- Point to **backpack** on page 8. Ask your child why **backpack** is a good name for a backpack. You could point out the meaning of each part of the word: back – the part of your body the bag is against; pack – bag.
- Read page 10, emphasising the rhyming sounds in **quill** and **Will**. Ask your child if they can think of a different name that rhymes with **quill**. (e.g. *Phil, Bill*)